The CHICKS' TRICK

by JENI BASSETT

COBBLEHILL BOOKS

Dutton · New York

Library of Congress Cataloging-in-Publication Data
Bassett, Jeni.
The chicks' trick / text and pictures by Jeni Bassett.
p.   cm.
Summary: Two hens, who love to compete against each other, insist
that each has the best chick.
ISBN 0-525-65152-7
[1. Chickens — Fiction.   2. Competition (Psychology) — Fiction.
3. Conduct of life — Fiction.]   I. Title.
PZ7.B2932Ch 1995
[E] — dc20   93-18471 CIP   AC

Published in the United States by Cobblehill Books,
an affiliate of Dutton Children's Books,
a division of Penguin Books USA Inc.,
375 Hudson Street, New York, New York 10014

Designed by Mina Greenstein
Printed in Hong Kong
First Edition   10   9   8   7   6   5   4   3   2   1

To my little chick, REBECCA,
hatched November 27, 1992

Mrs. Heckle and Mrs. Peckle were very proud hens.
They were always trying to outdo one another.

"Isn't my new hat wonderful?" asked Mrs. Heckle.

"Hummph," replied Mrs. Peckle. "Don't bother me. I'm busy making the best pink chiffon, chocolate swirl cake you've ever seen."

"We'll see about that," Mrs. Heckle said to herself.
She decided to make a super chocolate marshmallow,
butter brickle cake.

"Just look at *my* cake!" said Mrs. Heckle. "It is bigger than yours."

"Well, I'm sure mine tastes much better," replied Mrs. Peckle.

One day Mrs. Peckle declared that she had laid a perfect egg. "You should see how white and smooth and oval it is."

Not to be outdone, Mrs. Heckle laid an egg, too.
"Mine is spectacular!" she said. "There has never been
an egg so great."

"No, mine is better," Mrs. Peckle insisted. "My chick will be the best of all."

"I'm afraid not," said Mrs. Heckle.

They quarreled as they sat, and as they sat they quarreled.

Finally one day there was a cracking sound. Out popped a little chick.

"Why, my perfect egg has hatched the most beautiful chick in the world!" Mrs. Peckle cried. "I will call her Sweet Pea."

"But just look," said Mrs. Heckle. "My egg is hatching a wonderful downy chick, much better than yours. He will become a great rooster. I will name him Napoleon."

Next morning the chicks followed their mothers out into the barnyard. Mrs. Peckle said, "Look how fluffy Sweet Pea is." "Oh, but Napoleon is fluffier," Mrs. Heckle assured her.

"And Sweet Pea is so clever. Just see — she already knows how to scratch for a worm."

"Watch Napoleon. He has already caught a worm!"

The two argued and squabbled all day.

The two little chicks became friends while their mothers were busy arguing over which one was best. They played in the barnyard . . .

. . . catching bugs,

. . . leaping over puddles,

. . . and having a race.

They played Hide and Seek, and made up a game called
Find the Corn.

Their mothers continued to argue. "Did you see how Sweet
Pea catches bugs? She's so quick."

"She didn't catch that bug. Napoleon did."

The two chicks got tired of listening to their mothers argue all the time.

"Why don't we ask them to stop?" said Napoleon.

Sweet Pea agreed. They rolled a bucket to the middle of the yard. Napoleon climbed on top.

"No more arguing, please!" he said loudly.

"I'll stop arguing with her when she says I *do* have the prettiest chick," Mrs. Heckle clucked.

"And I'll stop arguing when she realizes *I* have the best chick," Mrs. Peckle said.

It all started again.

"Sweet Pea, I have an idea," whispered Napoleon.

"Let's play a trick," Napoleon said. And he told Sweet Pea
his plan. "We will switch places and see if they can tell the
difference."

That night when their mothers were asleep, the chicks
tiptoed out of their own nests and got into the other's nest.
The mothers did not wake up, and did not know they
had changed places.

Next morning Napoleon followed Mrs. Peckle around instead of his own mother. Sweet Pea followed Mrs. Heckle. The mother hens didn't notice which was which. They just continued to argue.

"My chick is much better," said Mrs. Peckle.

"Oh, but my chick is much more clever," said Mrs. Heckle.

Napoleon said to Sweet Pea, "Tonight we will *really* fool them."

That night Napoleon got into Mrs. Peckle's nest, and Sweet
Pea got into Mrs. Heckle's nest.

When the mother hens dozed off, the chicks made a lot of
noise while returning to their own nests. This time they wanted
to be sure their mothers knew they were changing places.

"They are trying to play a trick on us," Mrs. Heckle
thought.

"Sweet Pea thinks she can fool me by switching places," said
Mrs. Peckle to herself.

The next morning the two chicks winked at one another as
they followed their own mothers.

"Why, I declare, your chick *is* beautiful today," said Mrs.
Peckle, thinking it was Sweet Pea.

"Why, your chick is mighty pretty today, too," said Mrs.
Heckle, thinking she was talking about Napoleon.

"Look at those fluffy feathers and that nice sharp little beak," Mrs. Heckle said, looking at the chick following Mrs. Peckle.

Mrs. Heckle and Mrs. Peckle couldn't say enough nice things about the chick following the other one.

They didn't argue even once.

The two mothers decided to show off their chicks, and took them for a walk around the barnyard.

"Doesn't Mrs. Heckle have a nice chick?" Mrs. Peckle said to the ducks. But Mrs. Heckle quickly added, "Oh, no, Mrs. Peckle's chick is much prettier today."

When they met the pigs, the mothers continued to say nice things about the other's chick.

The mother pig had heard all the arguing and was glad not to have to listen to it anymore. "I really can't tell the difference," she said.

On the way back to the chicken yard, Mrs. Heckle and Mrs. Peckle agreed that it had been a lovely day.

At that, the two little chicks burst out laughing.

"What is so funny? Why are you laughing?" the mothers
wanted to know.

"You think we switched places last night," said Napoleon,
"but we were just getting back into our own nests. You both
have been praising the wrong chick all day long."

"Are you *sure*?" Mrs. Heckle and Mrs. Peckle asked.

"Of course, we are sure," Napoleon replied. "You didn't know when we changed places the first time."

"You just heard us when we were going back to our own nest," said Sweet Pea.

"And we thought we were outsmarting the two of you!" said Mrs. Peckle.

"Instead, you are the ones who fooled us," said Mrs. Heckle. They both started to laugh.

"You promised to stop arguing when each one said the other's chick was the best. Now you have done that," said Sweet Pea.

"So no more arguing," said Napoleon.

"No more arguing," the mother hens agreed.

"Mrs. Peckle, don't you think *both* our chicks are beautiful?"
"Indeed I do, Mrs. Heckle. And both are very clever."
From that day on, there was never another silly quarrel.

"You promised to stop arguing when each one said the other's chick was the best. Now you have done that," said Sweet Pea.

"So no more arguing," said Napoleon.

"No more arguing," the mother hens agreed.

"Mrs. Peckle, don't you think *both* our chicks are beautiful?"
"Indeed I do, Mrs. Heckle. And both are very clever."
From that day on, there was never another silly quarrel.